WHERE THE WORDS BEGIN

"COLLECTION OF QUIET LESSONS FROM THE MESS, THE MAGIC, AND THE MIDDLE OF IT ALL."

MANAL ZEESHAN

Contents

Preface

What joy is there in simply sitting by a window ledge, scribbling about a school trip I took when I was eight?

More than I ever imagined.

My relationship with words has always been more profound and intimate than a pastime. Paper has never just been paper to me. It has been a witness to my inner world, a quiet confidant that has held everything I didn't know how to say aloud. The blank page has absorbed my angst, my worries, my bursts of excitement, and every unspoken emotion a human heart can hold. Writing, for me, has never been just an activity. It has been a sanctuary. A place where I mend what feels broken, where I unravel confusion, and where I often find the courage to keep going. It has helped me navigate the blurry edges of life and guided me back to myself when I felt lost.

From easing the sting of a fight with my best friend to gently steering me toward my purpose, writing has always been the answer to my quietest "why."

I've always believed that the ability to translate emotions into words is one of the purest forms of art. It's a kind of magic, the kind that doesn't ask for applause. And for me, writing isn't just part of my life. It is me.

Growing up, there were days when I was surrounded by people, easily filling the space with conversation and laughter. But there were also days when I longed for something deeper, something real, when I searched for someone who saw the world the way I did, who understood that silence could also be loud. I have craved both solitude and connection at different points in my journey, and through it all, I've come to believe this: every meaningful exchange changes us. Every heartfelt conversation, every shared story, every unspoken moment of being seen or understood, leaves a mark. You never leave quite the same.

And that brings me to this book.

This is not a guidebook or a manual for how to live. It's a collection of lessons I'm still learning, stories that shaped me, and reflections that poured out when I had nowhere else to put them. It's drawn from conversations I've cherished, mistakes I've grown from, friendships I've held close, and ones I wish I had loved a little longer. It's stitched together from sleepless nights, quiet mornings, happy tears, aching ones, and everything in between.

This book is not about having it all figured out. If anything, it's about the beauty of not knowing, and choosing to keep showing up anyway.

I wrote this because I needed to. Because these words have lived in my heart for years, waiting for the right moment to find their way to someone else's. I wrote it for the younger version of me who needed reassurance that her voice mattered. And I wrote it for you, whoever you are, wherever you are, so you might find a piece of yourself in these pages, too.

More than anything, I hope this book feels like a conversation. A warm one. The kind that wraps around you like a soft blanket on a cold day. I hope you find a voice here that feels like your own. I hope you remember that your thoughts are valid, your story is worthy, and your way of seeing the world is enough. You don't need to be loud to be heard. You don't need to be perfect to be powerful.

Welcome to the beginning. This is where the words start, but the becoming, the unraveling, the healing... that's all you.

And that's enough.

I
No endings, No beginnings

"Some things don't start, they unfold. Like breath, like dawn, like becoming."

Why do full stops provoke such unease within us? Why does the mere idea of an ending make our hearts clench, our minds hesitate? Perhaps it's because we often mistake them for permanence when, in reality, they are merely commas in disguise, pauses, not conclusions. And yet, the fear of closure can paralyze us, making us cling to unfinished sentences, unresolved chapters, and moments that were never meant to last.

I used to see endings as a kind of defeat, a sign of surrender. I avoided them, convinced that if I ignored them long enough, I could rewrite the story in my favor. But life doesn't work that way. What I failed to realize was that some endings, no matter how uncomfortable, are necessary. Because endings, especially the painful ones, have a way of shaping us in ways we don't immediately understand. It has taken me countless sunrises to accept that while sunsets cast shadows and steal the light, they also make way for a new dawn. True brilliance is only appreciated when it emerges from the depths of darkness.

To truly live is to accept that life is unpredictable, relentless, and rarely gentle. It will not hand you what you desire simply because you want it. Instead, it will test you, stretch you beyond your limits, and challenge you to fight for what you believe in. The real question isn't whether life will be hard, it *will be*. The question is whether you will rise to meet it.

Failure has a way of seeping into our bones, of making us question everything we once believed in, our abilities, our dreams, even our faith. And let's be honest, when you're mentally overwhelmed, when disappointment grips you by the throat, it's nearly impossible to pause and reflect. In those moments, the weight of rejection feels insurmountable, the pain of loss unbearable. But if there is one thing I have learned, it is this: it is not the fall that defines you, it is how you rise.

A person who has the strength to embrace failure, to stand back up despite heartbreak, and to push forward with humility and resilience, that person is truly invincible. If you are shedding tears over a rejection, if your heart aches over something you poured your soul into, remember this: your setbacks are not proof of your inadequacy. They are the chisels shaping you into the person you are meant to become.

Life will break you. It will push you to the edge and demand to know if you dare to keep going. And in those moments, you must remind yourself that every ending, no matter how painful, carries the possibility of a beginning. It is in the spaces between what was and what will be that you discover who you truly are.

We often forget that life will never test us beyond what we are capable of enduring. It may stretch us, shake us, and push us to our absolute limits, but it will never break us, at least, not without also giving us the strength to rebuild. Accepting that something didn't work out is not an admission of defeat; it is a redirection toward something greater. But recognizing this truth requires more than just optimism, it takes resilience, patience, and the willingness to surrender to the unknown.

Life rarely gives us what we want; it gives us what we *need*. And because we don't always have the foresight to see the bigger picture, it can feel unbearably cruel in the moment. But those who learn to trust the process, to endure without demanding immediate answers, are the ones who ultimately emerge victorious.

The hardest lesson I've ever had to learn is that rejection is just redirection. When doors close, it stings. It feels personal, unfair, almost unbearable. But every single time, without fail, life has shown me that something greater was being orchestrated behind the scenes. Closed doors aren't the end of the road; they're stepping stones leading to something better. And when the right doors finally *do* open, you'll realize why the others had to remain shut.

I've had my fair share of "Why me, God?" moments, times when I felt like I was doing everything right, yet nothing seemed to go my way. But whenever I step back, even just for a moment, I see the undeniable truth: *I grow through what I go through.* Whether I win or lose, succeed or stumble, one thing remains constant: I evolve. Not just intellectually, but emotionally, spiritually, and in ways I could never have foreseen. And that, in itself, is a victory.

The sweetest victories are often preceded by the most painful setbacks. There have been moments when I felt utterly lost, questioning every decision, replaying every failure, wondering where I went wrong. But time has a way of revealing answers we weren't ready to hear before. I've learned that clarity doesn't always come in the moment; it comes in reflection, in quiet realizations, in the peace that follows after we've processed the storm.

And yet, as natural as it is to feel heartbroken when things don't go as planned, there's a fine line between feeling your pain and letting it consume you. It's okay to grieve what could have been, to sit with disappointment, to acknowledge that it hurts. But what's not okay is allowing that pain to blind you to what's still ahead. Life doesn't stop just because one chapter ends, and neither should you.

For the longest time, I struggled with detachment. I've always been an all-or-nothing person, fully invested, fully committed. And because of that, when things didn't work out, I took it personally. Whether it was a project, or a dream, I held on so tightly that the idea of letting go felt like losing a part of myself. But I'm learning, slowly but surely, that sometimes the real strength isn't in holding on, it's in loosening your grip and trusting the process.

The same applies to relationships. When friendships fade, bonds loosen, or people drift apart, it's easy to feel like you're the problem. Maybe you weren't enough. Maybe you don't know how to nurture relationships the way others do. I've had my lowest lows when it comes to the people I love, times when expectations didn't align, when distance grew without warning, when I gave too much and received too little. And no matter how many times it happens, it never gets easier.

We tend to place the heaviest blame on ourselves when it comes to the things closest to our hearts. But maybe, just maybe, not everything is ours to carry. I've spent years carrying burdens that were never mine, taking responsibility for things I had no control over. Every time a relationship hit a rough patch, I assumed it was entirely my fault. But if I can't control everything, then I shouldn't carry the weight of everything either.

Processing emotions is exhausting. It's overwhelming. And it's okay to have bad days, to cry over your mistakes, to sit with the discomfort of knowing some relationships just *won't* work out. What's *not* okay is shutting yourself off from the world, isolating yourself from opportunities, or making permanent decisions based on temporary pain. It's easy to retreat, to disconnect, to convince yourself that you're better off alone. But in the long run, that kind of self-protection is more draining than it is healing.

Speaking from a deeply personal space, I've come to believe that we need to trust in the timing of life. What is meant for you *will* find its way to you, whether it's a dream, a person, or an opportunity. And what isn't meant for you will fall away, no matter how tightly you try to hold on. I've spent too long blaming myself for every plan that unraveled, every relationship that changed, every loss I didn't see coming. And if there's one thing I've learned, it's this: *I shouldn't.*

Neither should you.

You are not defined by your setbacks. You are not less worthy because something didn't work out. You are not a failure because life took an unexpected turn. You are evolving in ways you may not understand yet. And one day, when the right doors open, when the right people walk into your life, when things *finally* fall into place, you'll understand why everything happened exactly as it did.

II

Get comfortable with being uncomfortable

"The soil never feels soft when seeds begin to split. Growth comes with pressure, with stretch, with ache. But oh, how the breaking leads to becoming."

Comfort is a quiet, seductive trap. It wraps itself around you like a warm blanket, familiar and reassuring. It convinces you that stillness is safety, that predictability is peace. But left unchecked, that very comfort can begin to harden into stagnation. What once felt like a sanctuary can become a cage.

I've learned this the hard way, by living in rooms I long outgrew, in routines that dulled my edges, in patterns I had long since mastered. When we become too settled in a particular place, rhythm, or way of thinking, a false sense of belonging can begin to feel like purpose. And that, I think, is one of the greatest tricks our minds play on us: equating comfort with meaning. Familiarity is not always alignment. Ease is not always growth.

I realized over time that I only truly come alive when I'm asked to stretch beyond what I know. When the universe nudges me, or sometimes shoves me out of whatever I've been clinging to too tightly. Left to my own devices, I can sleepwalk through life. But discomfort? That wakes me up.

And yet, here's the contradiction I live with: I crave growth, but I resist change. I want transformation, but I hate being nudged. I want to fly, but I cling to the ledge. The paradox frustrates me. How can I need discomfort to grow, but also fear it so deeply? I used to think something was wrong with me for feeling that way, but now I understand: this is what it means to be human. To want the reward without the risk. The breakthrough without the breakdown.

The truth is, success, when it comes too easily, can make me complacent. When everything falls into place without resistance, I stop trying as hard. I stopped asking deeper questions. I lost the urgency that once drove me. But failure? Rejection? Disappointment? Those things have a way of cracking me open. Of reintroducing me to myself. They force me to reevaluate, to confront the parts of me I would rather ignore, to grow in ways that comfort never demands.

I think there's something holy about that kind of disruption.

Discomfort has taught me more than success ever could. It's where I've found my grit, my voice, my resilience. It's where I've unearthed buried dreams and rebuilt broken confidence. It's where I've had to wrestle with hard truths, about myself, about others, about the world, and come out the other side with a deeper sense of who I am.

But none of this is easy. We don't leap toward discomfort with excitement. We tiptoe. We hesitate. And that's okay. You don't have to be fearless to grow. You just have to be willing.

Willing to take the first small step. To enter a room where you feel like you don't belong. To say yes to something that scares you. To speak when silence feels safer. To try, even if you're certain you'll fail.

I used to believe I didn't belong in certain rooms, that I wasn't qualified, charismatic, or confident enough. I whispered it to myself so often that it began to sound like the truth. But somewhere beneath that fear was a quieter voice, one that said, "Stay. Learn. Try anyway." And that's the voice I've been trying to listen to more often. Not because I feel worthy, but because I'm done letting fear decide where I do and don't belong.

Growth doesn't always look like triumph. Sometimes it looks like showing up to the meeting with your hands shaking. Sometimes it looks like finishing a task when your self-doubt is screaming. Sometimes it looks like staying in the room even when your heart says run. These moments don't look glamorous from the outside, but they are the foundation of every real transformation.

Confidence, contrary to what we're told, isn't something you're born with. It's something you build, layer by layer, choice by choice. It's not the absence of fear; it's the willingness to act despite it. Every person you admire for their confidence started exactly where you are: unsure, hesitant, filled with questions. The difference? They moved anyway.

And that's the magic. You don't have to wait for certainty to begin. You just have to move.

Some of the most defining moments of my life began with quiet, reluctant courage. The job I applied for, even though I thought I wasn't good enough. The idea I spoke aloud, even when I was afraid of sounding foolish. The decision to walk into unfamiliar spaces with nothing but a shaky sense of hope. Every time I stepped forward, I discovered a piece of myself I didn't know was there.

Discomfort is not the enemy. It's the invitation. The door. The threshold between who you are and who you're becoming.

Most people stay stuck not because they lack talent or passion, but because they've made a home out of comfort. They wait for clarity, for the perfect moment, for some magical sign that it's time. But clarity doesn't come from thinking, it comes from doing. The longer you sit on the sidelines, the more power fear gains. But the moment you step forward, even just a little, the fear begins to lose its grip.

It's not about being fearless. It's about being honest. Honest enough to admit that you're scared, and brave enough to move anyway.

We often underestimate the power of small steps. Sitting next to someone new. Asking a question you don't know the answer to. Trying a thing you might be terrible at. These things seem insignificant, but they build something far more important than confidence: they build character. They build self-trust. They teach you that even when things don't go perfectly, you'll survive. And more than that, you'll grow.

So here's what I'm learning to do: invite discomfort in like an old friend. Not because I enjoy it, but because I trust what it brings out of me. It keeps me humble. It keeps me hungry. It keeps me becoming.

Because on the other side of discomfort is someone stronger. Wiser. More grounded. More alive.

And she's worth meeting.

III

You are everything you have

The world didn't end when that friendship you swore would last forever quietly fell apart, leaving only a string of memories and silence where laughter used to live. It didn't stop spinning the moment you found yourself sitting alone at the back of the classroom, feigning interest in your notebook just to keep from facing the sting of being left out. It kept turning, relentlessly, indifferently, even on those nights when you stared at your phone, heart heavy with the realization that they went out without you, again. And it certainly didn't come crashing down when you lay in bed, staring at the ceiling through tear-blurred eyes, feeling the ache of loneliness in your chest so real, it felt like a second heartbeat.

And still, through it all, you carried yourself. That's the part no one talks about. The quiet resilience. The way you held yourself when no one else did. The strength it took to simply keep going when it felt like the world had turned its back on you.

We underestimate that kind of power. The kind that doesn't need applause or recognition. The kind that exists in whispered pep talks and tear-streaked promises to try again tomorrow. We talk so much about needing others, about finding our people, about love, about community, and yes, those things matter deeply. But what about the strength it takes to hold your own hand when no one's reaching for it? What about the kind of love that begins with self-acceptance, with learning to be your own sanctuary?

Why are we so afraid of being alone?

Loneliness is one of the most feared emotions we face, but I've come to believe that it isn't the absence of others that haunts us most. It's the absence of ourselves. The ache comes not just from being without someone, but from forgetting that we were never incomplete to begin with. You only feel truly alone when you begin to believe that you are not enough for yourself.

The urge to run to someone else, to fill that void with attention or validation, often comes from a fracture within, a place where self-trust has worn thin. We don't fear solitude; we fear what we'll hear in the silence. But silence doesn't mean emptiness. It means space. Space to hear your own voice again. Space to rebuild without needing permission. Space to breathe, to become, to belong to yourself.

We often think the real heartbreak is when people leave. But the true loss is when we stop believing in our own presence. When we begin to see our worth as a condition, based on who stays, who notices, and who calls. When we forget that our value isn't something others confirm, it's something we carry.

Yes, we need people. We need shared laughter, knowing glances, hands to hold when the weight is too much. We are wired for connection. But we don't just need people, we need the right people. The ones who mirror our strength, not magnify our insecurities. The ones who water our growth, not question our worth.

And if the people around you diminish your light more than they reflect it, ask yourself: are you keeping them in your life out of love, or out of fear? Fear of being alone. Fear of facing yourself. Fear that you are not enough without them.

But here's the truth: there is nothing more powerful than standing tall in your solitude. When you learn to be at peace in your own company, when you stop chasing half-hearted connections just to feel full, you discover a kind of freedom that can't be shaken.

Because once you know how to carry yourself, you realize you have nothing to lose.

I've had nights where I felt the ground disappear beneath me. Mornings when I woke up with a hollow ache I couldn't name. But one thought always pulled me back from the edge: *I have been here before. I have survived this ache before. I am enough, with or without a safety net.*

Having people to lean on is beautiful. Cherish it. Hold it close. But understand this: there will be days when no one shows up. When the phone doesn't ring. When the room feels too big and your heart too heavy. And on those days, you will learn what it means to be your own anchor.

You'll learn that strength isn't just loud. Sometimes, strength is quiet. It's brushing your teeth after crying all night. It's sending the message even though your hands are shaking. It's getting up again, after failing. It's sitting with your pain without letting it define you.

There will be people who walk beside you on your brightest days. But the people who matter most are the ones who stand by you when the lights go out, and that includes *you.*

Because when no one else is clapping, will you still cheer for yourself?

When no one's validating your worth, will you still believe in it?

When no one is offering you comfort, will you still choose to be gentle with yourself?

Those questions matter. Because life is unpredictable. There will be days when love shows up in arms that hold you, and days when love shows up in the simple act of you keeping yourself together. And both are worthy. Both are enough.

So on the days when you feel invisible, remind yourself: *I am seen, by me.*

On the days when you feel too small, whisper: *I am enough, as I am.*

On the days when you're tempted to shrink to fit someone's comfort, say: *I was never made to be less.*

When you hit rock bottom, and you will, it won't be the end. It'll be the foundation. The place where you rebuild with intention. With clarity. With strength that's no longer borrowed but built.

Each night you go to sleep, you won't just be older. You'll be stronger. Because every single day you've made it through pain, silence, doubt, and fear, you've proven something unshakable:

You have always had you.

So cherish yourself. Not just on the good days. Especially on the hard ones. Celebrate your ability to survive, to heal, to keep believing in yourself when no one else knew how. Be your own safe place. Be your own reminder. Be your own light.

You can either be your biggest critic or your fiercest defender. It's a choice. One you make again and again.

And when you choose yourself fully, without condition, you give yourself the greatest gift there is: *unwavering, unconditional acceptance.*

That's what will carry you through the storms. Not the promise of never falling, but the quiet, steady conviction that even if you do, you'll rise.

Because you always have.

And you always will.

IV
Yesterday builds Tomorrow

"We are stitched together by the days we thought we wouldn't survive."

Why do our present actions feel so intricately tethered to memories, echoes of conversations we can't seem to forget, versions of ourselves we no longer are but still mourn? We scroll through old messages, retrace our steps, and replay the things we said, or didn't say, like a song on loop, hoping that somehow, by remembering it hard enough, we might be able to soften the ache of what can't be undone.

But here's the question I keep circling back to:

Why is our obsession with the past always painted in shades of regret?

Why is it seen as a weakness to linger in thought, to hold space for the people we once were? We're told to *let go*, to *move on*, to *stop overthinking*. As if reflection is a detour. As if thinking deeply about what hurt us means we're stuck. But isn't growth born from reflection? Isn't the best kind of evolution the one that honors where we've been, not just where we're going?

I remember a day that still sits heavy in my memory, one of those quiet, ordinary afternoons that became a turning point without asking permission.

I was brushing my hair, standing in front of the mirror. Nothing dramatic. Just another day. But as I looked at myself, really looked, I saw someone I didn't quite recognize. Someone is exhausted from trying to be okay. Someone haunted by all the things she wished she could've done differently. I don't remember what exactly triggered it, maybe a conversation I had earlier that week, maybe an old photo I had scrolled past on my phone, but that day, my reflection didn't feel like a reflection. It felt like a confrontation.

It was the first time I realized how many versions of me were still living in that mirror. Versions that hadn't forgiven themselves. That hadn't healed. That hadn't stopped carrying the weight of what was long gone. And for the first time, I didn't look away. I didn't try to smile through it or push past it. I just stood there and let myself feel it all.

I've always been the kind of person who feels deeply and processes slowly. The kind who realizes their mistakes after the damage has already settled. The kind who lies awake at night, replaying conversations like old film reels, haunted by words I wish I could take back and moments I wish I could redo.

For the longest time, I believed this made me weak. That my inability to "move on" with grace and speed meant I was broken. The past had more control over me than it should have.

But I've come to understand something I wish I had known sooner:

Reflection is not the enemy.

Self-condemnation is.

It's not wrong to look back. It's not wrong to miss things, to mourn what could have been, to hold space for the people and choices that shaped you. What becomes harmful is when you weaponize your memories, when you punish yourself for not knowing what you know now.

The truth is, we don't always get it right the first time. Some mistakes take years to unravel. Some wounds need more than insight, they need time. Some lessons won't make sense until the fifth or sixth time we revisit them.

Growth is not forgetting the past. It's carrying it differently. It's choosing to visit the past with compassion, not judgment.

Mirrors don't lie, but they don't tell the whole story either.

They show the version of you that exists in this single moment. But they don't reveal how far you've come, what you've survived, or how many nights you held yourself together in silence. They don't reflect the weight you've shed, the burdens you've outgrown, or the internal wars you've quietly won.

So if you're someone who's constantly looking back, wondering why you can't just "get over it", this is for you:

You're not stuck. You're sifting.

You're not broken. You're building.

You're not behind. You're becoming.

Let go of what no longer serves you, but only after you've truly absorbed its lesson. Only after you've honored it for what it was and released it for what it can no longer be. There's nothing noble in clinging to pain just because it's familiar. But there's nothing weak about needing time to outgrow it either.

Give yourself the grace to be a work in progress.

To falter. To feel too much. To learn the hard way. To revisit the same lesson until it finally clicks. Healing isn't linear. Sometimes it loops. Sometimes it takes the long way. Sometimes it repeats itself until you realize the wound was never the problem; your refusal to face it was.

You're allowed to outgrow who you used to be without hating who you were.

Life has a way of feeling unbearably heavy when the weight of the past overshadows the promise of the future. But in the endless tug-of-war between who you were and who you want to be, don't forget where your power actually lives: **here.**

Right now. This breath. This heartbeat.

Not in a future version of you who's already healed.

Not in the person who never made the mistake in the first place.

But in you, today, with your messy thoughts, aching heart, and quiet hope.

Because this is where change begins, not once everything is fixed, but while things are still falling into place. This is the moment where you decide what kind of story you want to write next.

And if you're still haunted by things you wish you had done differently, remind yourself: **you're allowed to begin again, even if you've already begun a hundred times before.**

One day, you'll look in the mirror again, and you won't see regret.

You'll see resilience.

You'll see someone who chose to face the pain rather than numb it. Someone who loved deeply, hurt deeply, and still chose to grow anyway. Someone who didn't rush the process, who stayed with their becoming, who turned reflection into redemption.

So be patient with your healing. Be gentle with your past. And be proud of the strength it takes to sit with your own story and say,

"I am not my mistakes. I am the person who learned from them."

Ask yourself:

- What version of me still lives in the mirror, waiting to be forgiven?
- What lesson has the past been trying to teach me over and over?
- What weight am I carrying that I no longer need to hold?

These questions don't require perfect answers. Just honest ones.

Let the mirror show you not just who you are, but who you're still becoming.

And when you forget, when the past feels louder than your future, come back here. To this page. To this promise:

You are not stuck. You are sifting.

You are not broken. You are building.

You are not behind. You are becoming.

V
Give Yourself a Break

"Even the sun rests behind clouds without apology; why shouldn't you?"

It's no surprise that even when our bodies are still, our minds rarely follow suit. We are perpetual thinkers, planners, and overanalyzers, carrying the weight of our ambitions, regrets, and uncertainties at all times. Even in sleep, our minds remain restless, sifting through dreams, reliving failures, replaying conversations that ended too soon or stretched too long. I remember one evening in particular, exhausted after a week of pushing through deadlines and expectations, I sat on the bathroom floor, back against the cold tile, and cried. It wasn't a dramatic, heaving sob. Just quiet, tired tears. I didn't even know what I was crying about. That's the thing about burnout, it doesn't always announce itself with sirens. Sometimes it arrives as numbness, as silence, as the inability to answer a simple "How are you?" without breaking down. I felt guilty for feeling tired, as if I hadn't earned my exhaustion, as if rest was something to be deserved, not needed. But that moment taught me something: even strong people crack. And that crack? It's not the end, it's the space where light can enter.

We exist in a world that glorifies productivity, where rest is often mistaken for laziness, and burnout is worn like a badge of honor. The pressure to keep moving, to stay ahead, to always be "on" isn't just an expectation; it's a necessity in the race toward success. But at what cost? Here's what I've learned: we have one life, and none of us has a handbook on how to navigate it perfectly. It's okay to stumble, to struggle with emotions, to not always have the answers. It's okay to feel like giving up. And sometimes, it's not just okay, it's necessary to pause, to breathe, to step back before pushing forward again. Rest isn't weakness, it's fuel. Crying it out, admitting you're overwhelmed, taking a break from work, or just lying in bed without is feeling the need to justify it, these are not signs of failure. They are acts of self-preservation. There is a fine line between discipline and self-punishment, and learning to differentiate the two is one of the most valuable lessons we can teach ourselves.

What is the point of relentless hard work if it drains you to the point where you no longer recognize yourself? A healthy grind is one where passion fuels consistency, not where exhaustion depletes it. If you find yourself burning out too quickly, it's not because you lack drive; it's because you lack balance. Listen to your body. Pay attention to your mind. I wish I could say I've mastered the art of balance, but I haven't. I've pushed myself to extremes, working past exhaustion, numbing my emotions to keep going, convincing myself that resting meant I was falling behind. And other times, I've let myself slip too far into comfort, mistaking avoidance for self-care. The truth is, finding that middle ground is a struggle, especially for those of us who are all-or-nothing people.

I remember scrolling through social media one night while lying in bed, eyes burning from the screen, feeling like the whole world was moving forward without me. Everyone seemed to be doing more, being more, succeeding more. Meanwhile, I was frozen in place, mentally and emotionally drained. But here's what comparison never shows you: the hidden breakdowns behind curated smiles. I wasn't falling behind. I was just in a season of rebuilding. A quiet, internal season that wasn't glamorous but was necessary. You are allowed to feel it all. The good days that make you laugh and the bad days that make you want to disappear. The mornings where you wake up ready to take on the world and the ones where getting out of bed is the only victory you can manage. Both are valid. Both are human.

From the moment we learn what emotions are, we're taught how to chase happiness. But what we really need to learn is how to sit with our sadness, how to honor our struggles without shame, how to extend kindness to ourselves when we are at our lowest. Because why should every day begin with the pressure to conquer the world? Some days, it's enough to simply exist. So take the pause. Breathe. Love yourself when you're thriving, but love yourself even more when you're not. The world will be quick to tell you that you're not enough, but slow to acknowledge your victories. That's just how it is. So be your own advocate. Celebrate yourself. Forgive yourself. Be gentle. It's a tough world, one that will push you down if you let it. So hold your ground. Cry if you need to, but don't stay in the breakdown. Pick yourself up, take it slow, take it steady, and keep going.

Why do we cling so fiercely to the yesteryears of our lives? Why do our present actions seem tethered to the echoes of what has already passed? We mourn lost moments, replay conversations, and dissect old decisions as if somehow, through sheer will, we can rewrite what's already been written. But here's the question I keep coming back to: why is this obsession with the past always framed as something negative? Isn't growth a process of reflection? Isn't the best kind of evolution the one where our present self takes the lessons of yesterday and uses them to shape a wiser, stronger tomorrow? I've always been the kind of person who makes mistakes, realizes them too late, and regrets them even faster. I replay moments, wondering how different things could have been if I had just acted sooner, spoken differently, or chosen another path. And for the longest time, I saw this as a flaw. I believed that my inability to simply "let go" made me weak. But now, I'm beginning to understand that reflection is not the enemy; self-condemnation is.

The truth is, we can't always fix things in an instant. Some mistakes take time to unravel. Some lessons take years to sink in. But what we can do is reflect, learn, and move forward with greater awareness. We can acknowledge where we went wrong, not to punish ourselves, but to ensure we don't repeat the same cycles. Growth isn't about forgetting the past, it's about using it as a foundation for a better future. So, shift your mindset. Let go of what no longer serves you, but only after you've truly absorbed its lesson. Give yourself the grace to be human, to falter, to stumble, to be a work in progress. Stop punishing yourself for not always getting it right the first time. Mistakes don't define you. The way you rise from them does.

Life has a way of feeling unbearably heavy, especially when the weight of the past threatens to overshadow your future. But in the endless push-and-pull between yesterday and tomorrow, don't lose sight of the power you hold in the present. Because right now, this moment, is where change begins. And if you need the reminder, you've got what it takes. Go for that walk, climb that mountain, dive into the ocean, or simply sit in the quiet and let yourself be. Witness the sunrise at 4 a.m., watch the sunset from your window, or do absolutely nothing at all. This life is yours to live, and only you can decide when to push and when to pause. No one else will do it for you.

VI
Fake it till you make it

"Wear the confidence before it fits. One day, it will."

Perfection is a mirage, glimmering in the distance like a promise we can almost touch. We chase it with conviction, convinced that once we arrive, once we become that flawless version of ourselves, we will finally feel worthy. But the closer we draw to it, the further it seems to dissolve into the horizon. And in that chase, we lose more than time, we lose ourselves. We measure our worth against the impossible, and when we inevitably fall short, we crumble, not just under the weight of disappointment but under the quiet ache of shame.

But the truth, the quiet, life-altering truth, is this: you were never meant to be perfect. You were meant to be real.

Messy. Beautifully flawed. In progress.

It's okay if your voice shakes when you speak, if your steps are unsure, if your dreams feel both too big and not enough all at once. It's okay if your mirror reflects more doubt than confidence. You are not broken for feeling this way. You are human.

That's the thing, we equate progress with poise, with power, with polished final drafts. But the truth is, growth is often found in the in-between. In the unedited. In the unfinished.

One of the most humbling things I've learned is that self-worth isn't built in the spotlight, it's nurtured in the quiet. In the choice to show up when no one's watching. In the courage to begin again after every misstep.

You don't have to be the loudest voice in the room to be heard. You don't have to carry the elegance of a poet, the brilliance of a scholar, or the confidence of someone who seems perpetually unshaken. You just have to be willing to be you.

And being you? That's the work of a lifetime.

I used to think confidence was something bestowed on the chosen few, something you were either born with or not. But now I see it as a slow unfolding. A thousand tiny decisions to keep going despite the inner voices that say you shouldn't. It's walking into a room even when your knees tremble. Speaking your truth even when your voice cracks. Showing up again and again, not because you feel ready, but because you believe that somewhere inside you, you're becoming ready.

Confidence isn't the absence of doubt. It's choosing not to let doubt stop you.

And perfection? That's not the goal anymore. Wholeness is. Authenticity is. Becoming isn't about proving yourself, it's about meeting yourself where you are, with compassion and honesty.

There's a delicate balance between pushing yourself toward growth and punishing yourself for not being further along. I've been on both ends of that spectrum. I've glorified overworking to the point of depletion. I've drowned in the noise of comparison, shrinking under the weight of everyone else's highlight reel. I've let the silence between accomplishments convince me I was falling behind.

But I've also learned to catch myself. To pull back. To breathe. And more importantly, to rewrite the stories I tell myself when things don't go as planned.

Self-improvement isn't supposed to feel like self-erasure. And discipline, when it turns into self-denial, stops being noble and starts becoming cruel. Growth should never require abandoning your own humanity.

There's a kind of quiet strength in gentleness, in being kind to yourself on the days when everything feels heavy. There's a power in saying, "Today, this is enough," and meaning it.

I think about all the times I didn't give myself that grace. When I let shame masquerade as motivation. When I told myself I had to earn rest, earn love, earn the right to just exist. And yet, in hindsight, those were the days I needed love the most, not because I had done something extraordinary, but because I hadn't.

Let this be your reminder: you don't need to hustle for your worth. You don't need to apologize for needing rest. And you certainly don't need to be perfect to be worthy of love, belonging, or peace.

The people who seem to "have it all together" often aren't the ones who never fall; they're the ones who've learned how to rise, softly and steadily, after each stumble. They've learned that self-love isn't the reward at the end of the journey. It's the foundation that makes the journey possible.

So when the world demands more of you than you have to give, give yourself grace. When your reflection doesn't match your expectations, offer yourself kindness. And when you doubt your place in this world, return to this truth: you are not here to be perfect. You are here to be real, to be growing, to be becoming.

Becoming isn't a destination, it's a devotion. A quiet, relentless returning to yourself.

Again and again.

And that, more than anything, is enough.

VII

Built in the Quiet, Not the Headlines

"Growth isn't always a spotlight moment, it's a quiet unfolding."

Words are easy. They fill the air effortlessly, softening silences, creating illusions of certainty, painting visions of change. But words, as powerful as they may seem, do not build lives. They do not mend what is broken. They do not mold character, nor do they create the momentum needed to transform a life. It is not the speech that changes the course of a journey, it's the steady, sometimes silent, steps we take.

I've learned, often the hard way, that declarations are easy; persistence is hard. That promises can be made in seconds, but kept only through seasons of showing up when it's inconvenient, unglamorous, and unrewarded. The truth is, real growth doesn't happen in a flash of inspiration. It doesn't arrive with applause or grand announcements. It happens in the quiet, private corners of life, when no one is watching.

There was a time when I believed in the magic of saying things out loud, as if voicing a dream was the same as chasing it. I would fill journals with plans, voice notes with affirmations, conversations with conviction. I thought if I said the right things, enough times, something in the universe would shift and carry me forward. But more often than not, I found myself stuck. Because saying is not the same as doing.

The ones who truly move mountains rarely talk about it as they're doing it. They're too busy climbing.

And the ones who talk the loudest? They are often the ones who fear the silence, the weight of actually having to begin.

Nature taught me this. The sun never boasts of its brilliance, yet it shows up every morning, quietly dependable, spilling light over the world. Trees do not narrate their endurance, yet they weather every season, their roots growing deeper in silence. And the waves? They do not proclaim their persistence, yet they shape shorelines simply by returning, over and over again.

So why do we, as humans, feel such an aching need to explain ourselves? Why do we reveal our goals before they've had the chance to breathe? Why do we chase the validation of others before we've validated ourselves?

For years, I tried to convince people of who I was becoming. I explained myself tirelessly, every plan, every pivot, every change of heart. I wanted people to understand me, to see me clearly, to believe in my intentions. I thought if they saw me trying, they would offer the acceptance I hadn't yet given myself.

But the truth is, some people will misunderstand you no matter how eloquently you explain. Some will doubt you simply because they've never dared to try. Some will root for your failure because your courage reminds them of their own hesitation.

So I stopped performing. I stopped announcing and started building.

I began to show up for myself, not for approval, not for applause, but because I finally understood that the most important promise I could keep was the one I made to myself.

It wasn't easy. I still faltered. I still had days when I wanted to be seen, days when I questioned whether all the effort mattered if no one noticed. But over time, something quiet and beautiful began to grow: self-trust.

I started small. Waking up when I said I would. Writing when I didn't feel like it. Choosing action over avoidance. Not perfect action, but honest, human, humble steps. I stopped treating setbacks like failure and started seeing them as proof that I was trying. And something shifted. I began to rely on myself, to believe my own momentum. That changed everything.

Because here's the thing: validation is addictive, but fleeting. It gives you a rush, but it doesn't last. And when the high fades, you're left hollow unless you've built something more substantial, something internal. That something is self-trust.

Some of the most meaningful chapters of your life will be written in silence. No audience. No recognition. Just you, showing up, even when you'd rather disappear. Just you, doing the work, even when no one claps. Just you, becoming.

That's where the magic happens.

Not in grand speeches, but in ordinary days. Not in telling the world what you'll do, but in becoming the kind of person who does it, quietly, steadily, without needing permission or praise.

So if you find yourself on the path and no one seems to notice, keep going.

If you feel unseen, unacknowledged, uncelebrated... keep going.

If you're making changes that no one else understands... keep going.

Because the most powerful transformations don't require fanfare. They don't need hashtags or witnesses or status updates. They need consistency. They need patience. They need belief.

And when the results finally arrive, when the world begins to notice what you've built brick by silent brick, you won't need to say a word. Your life will speak for itself.

Just don't forget: the most important eyes watching your journey are your own.

Keep showing up for them.

VIII

I'm Faster, But She's the Fastest

**"Not every race is meant to be won.
Some are meant to teach you how to stay in your lane without shrinking."**

"I'm faster, but she's the fastest."

At first glance, it's a throwaway line, a humble nod, a quiet acknowledgment. But tucked inside those simple words is something more intricate. It's a window into how we often dilute our own accomplishments the moment we hold them up beside someone else's. It's subtle, almost unnoticeable, like a shadow that trails behind us without ever making a sound. But it's there. That whisper of self-doubt. That question we rarely voice aloud: *Am I enough if someone else is more?*

I remember a moment in school, standing at the edge of the track after finishing second in a race I had trained for months. My heart was pounding from the effort, but my mind was somewhere else entirely, focused not on how far I'd come, but on how far ahead someone else was. She was faster. Her time was better. Her name would be announced, not mine. And just like that, the pride I'd felt during the final stretch evaporated, replaced by a quiet sense of not-quite-there.

It's strange, isn't it? How quickly we shrink our joy.

We achieve something beautiful, something we once only dreamed of, and instead of honoring it, we dim its light. We scan the room, the feed, the leaderboard, looking for someone who did it bigger, better, cleaner, quicker. And we find them. We always find them. Because someone else's highlight reel will always make our behind-the-scenes look less polished.

But why do we do this to ourselves?

Competition, when wielded gently, can be a catalyst. It can inspire us, fuel our discipline, and challenge us to stretch beyond what we believed possible. But comparison, especially the kind rooted in insecurity, is far more dangerous. It's a slow erosion of self-worth, disguised as ambition. Unlike healthy competition, which pushes us to grow, comparison pushes us to question whether growth even matters if it doesn't come with applause.

There's a fine line, thinner than we think, between striving and spiraling. Between motivation and obsession. Between being inspired by others and feeling diminished by them.

I've found myself tiptoeing along that line more times than I care to admit. Sometimes, I'd accomplish something I was genuinely proud of, a good grade, a personal best, a creative breakthrough, and then I'd stumble across someone who had done it all, only more. Their success wasn't just visible, it was loud, celebrated, and broadcast. And suddenly, my own triumphs felt muted, like background noise in someone else's symphony.

But here's what I've had to learn, over and over, gently and sometimes painfully:

Someone else's greatness doesn't make yours any smaller.

It's not a finite resource. There's no cosmic scoreboard tallying who's ahead. The path is not a race, and success is not a medal that gets handed to the one with the fewest stumbles.

The truth is, no one can take away your progress. No one can rewrite the hours you spent trying, failing, and showing up again. The only person who can discredit your journey... is you. When you let someone else's finish line overshadow the distance you've traveled.

We're taught early on that success lives at the top of the class, the podium, the list. But what about the person who started at the bottom and kept climbing? What about the one who failed and still found the courage to begin again? Why isn't that the story we celebrate?

The most radical shift I've experienced is redefining what success looks like for me. Not in relation to anyone else. Not filtered through the lens of what I should be by now. But measured by growth, resilience, and the simple fact that I am still trying, still becoming.

I think about the people I admire most, and it's not because they were always the best. It's because they were honest. Because they fell and didn't hide the bruises. Because they didn't let comparison steal their love for what they were building. Their joy was not conditional. It was rooted in something internal, unwavering.

We all have something like that, something we loved before we worried about being good at it. A passion, a pursuit, a quiet joy. Maybe it was writing, or dancing, or painting, or singing off-key in the car. Something that made you feel more alive. More you. Until one day, someone else was better at it, and suddenly, it didn't feel like yours anymore.

But here's the thing: it still is. It always was.

Joy isn't a competition. And fulfillment can't be ranked.

When you measure your growth only in comparison to others, you miss the beauty of becoming. The quiet strength it takes to keep going without recognition. The courage it takes to show up as you are, not as the polished version you think the world prefers.

There is no final destination. No perfect version of yourself waiting at the end of the road. Life will always present someone who's further along, who's more applauded, who seems to have figured it out faster. That doesn't mean you're behind. It just means your journey is unfolding at its own pace.

And maybe that's the most freeing truth of all: you don't have to win to be proud. You don't have to prove to be valid. You don't have to be "the best" to be worthy.

You just have to keep becoming, your way, your time, your rhythm.

Let your success be quiet if it needs to be. Let it be slow. Let it be imperfect. Just don't let it be forgotten. Don't forget to celebrate what you once only hoped for. Don't forget to hold space for your own progress.

Because the moment you stop trying to outshine others and start trying to outgrow who you were, that's when the real magic happens.

So if you find yourself comparing, come back to your why. Come back to the feeling that started it all. Remind yourself that joy doesn't need to be earned. That becoming isn't about being better than someone else, it's about becoming more of who you already are.

IX

What the Easy Road Could Never Teach You

"No one truly enjoys the rush of running downhill until they've fought their way up."

What comes easily rarely shapes us. Ease may comfort, but it does not carve. It does not stretch or strengthen. It merely soothes, and while soothing has its place, it is not the birthplace of growth.

We all crave comfort in one way or another. We dream of soft landings, of doors that swing open without resistance, of days when everything simply works. And yet, again and again, it is the uphill climbs, the restless nights, the trembling moments of uncertainty that leave their mark. Not the moments that go smoothly, but the ones that demand something from us, something deeper, something truer.

Struggle, unwelcome as it may be, is life's most honest teacher. It arrives uninvited, often unannounced, and stays longer than we'd like. It doesn't flatter or sugarcoat. It confronts us, brutally, beautifully, with the edges of who we are. The raw corners. The unfinished places.

And still, we look at others and wonder why our path feels more jagged, more uphill. We compare our muddy trail to someone else's polished highlight reel and forget that every mountain peak casts its own kind of shadow. It's easy to romanticize someone else's ascent when you haven't seen the blisters on their feet.

But here's the truth: life is not fair. It never promised to be. While you are catching your breath halfway up your mountain, someone else might be dancing in the sun at their summit. While you are doubting your next step, someone else seems to be gliding. And it hurts. That kind of quiet comparison, that silent ache of "why is it harder for me?", it's real.

But life was never meant to be a straight line, nor a race with equal lanes. Your terrain is different because your story demands it. Because your becoming requires it. And though it may not feel like it in the moment, the unevenness of your road is not a punishment, it's a preparation.

You are not defined by the ease of your victories but by the resilience of your return. Success is not the truest measure of your strength; failure is. The breaking moments, the collapsed hopes, the days you barely made it out of bed, those are the places where your truest self was forged. Where character takes shape not in applause, but in the silence after defeat.

It is in the aching, lonely middle that we discover our essence. In the absence of witnesses, we learn who we are when there's no one left to impress. When there is only our own breath, and the question: will I try again?

Pain strips away the noise. It brings us face-to-face with what remains when the distractions dissolve. It is not noble, nor poetic in real time. It stings. It isolates. But it also chisels. It sculpts us into people who feel deeply, love harder, and walk into the fire again, not because they want to suffer, but because they have learned they can survive.

We often confuse strength with stillness. We imagine it as stoic, composed, untouched by the chaos around us. But real strength is not the absence of feeling, it's the courage to feel everything fully and still choose to rise. It is crying and continuing. It is breaking and rebuilding. It is admitting that you are struggling, and yet still reaching for the next rung on the ladder.

Strength is refusing to harden when the world tries to make you brittle. It is vulnerability turned inside out, grit in the form of softness.

I have learned, sometimes the hardest way, that being fully, unapologetically myself is not a weakness. It is the most radical act of self-respect. And in a world that profits off your self-doubt, choosing to embrace your full, flawed humanity is nothing short of rebellion.

Growth is not about perfecting, it's about persisting. It's not about pretending to be unshaken, but about learning to move through the shaking. About falling in love with the process, even when the process is painful.

So yes, cry if you must. Let the tears fall without shame. Break down if you need to. Let yourself fall apart, knowing you can rebuild. Speak your truth, even if your voice trembles, especially then.

And above all, keep going.

Because life will not hand you anything easy. It will not pause for your pain. It will challenge you at every turn. But it will also shape you, if you let it. It will not always be kind, but it will be honest. And in its honesty, it will invite you to become something greater than comfort could ever produce.

So the question remains: will you let the weight of it all break you, or will you let it make you? Will you follow the well-worn path of safety, or will you carve out a trail of your own, imperfect and courageous?

This life, the one that tests you, unmakes you, demands everything from you, is not the enemy. It is your forge.

And the person who comes out on the other side of the fire?

She's someone the easy road could never have created.

X
Start where you are

Let's be real, no one ever feels completely ready.

Not truly. Not deep in their bones. There's no divine thunderclap announcing that it's time to leap, no sacred whisper confirming that you are finally enough. Most of the time, beginnings feel terrifyingly premature. We step forward with shaky hands, pounding hearts, and minds full of noise, what if I'm not good enough, what if I fail, what if I make a fool of myself?

But here's the quiet truth no one tells you: *readiness is a myth.* It isn't something we wait for. It isn't something bestowed upon us when we've reached some arbitrary threshold of confidence or competence. Readiness is something we *build*, brick by brick, breath by breath, step by uncertain step.

Still, we hesitate. We convince ourselves that we need to be more, more polished, more experienced, more perfect, before we are "allowed" to start. But that's like holding a seed in one hand and an oak tree in the other, then scoffing at the seed for not being tall enough. Growth doesn't apologize for its slow unfolding. It doesn't rush to meet the expectations we've attached to it. It simply *begins*, small, fragile, but full of potential.

The people we admire, the ones who seem to glide effortlessly through life with clarity and grace, didn't start that way. They weren't born knowing how to lead, how to create, how to speak with conviction. They began where we all begin: uncertain, afraid, often alone with their dreams. The difference? They started anyway.

Starting something new is always a risk. It means stepping into the unknown. It means betting on yourself when the outcome is still a question mark. And often, it means doing so in the shadow of self-doubt, where every move feels like it's being made under a spotlight of imagined judgment.

I know this feeling intimately. I've stood on the threshold of something I deeply wanted and convinced myself I wasn't ready. I've delayed projects for months, even years, not because I lacked ability, but because I was waiting for the fear to go away. But fear doesn't dissolve with time. It softens only with motion.

Life doesn't hand us confidence on a silver platter. Confidence is something we *earn* through showing up. Not once, not when we feel at our best, but again and again, especially when we feel uncertain. Especially when our hands are shaking and our voice cracks and our heart whispers, *you're not ready yet.*

But here's the thing: no one gets to skip the shaky beginning. No one gets to arrive at mastery without enduring the awkward, uncertain firsts. The real tragedy isn't failing, it's never starting at all. Because when you don't begin, you rob yourself of the chance to become the person you were meant to be.

We often think that waiting protects us, that by holding off until we're more prepared, we're being smart, responsible, safe. But in reality, hesitation comes with a cost. The opportunities we let pass don't vanish into the void; they become someone else's breakthrough. The door you stand before, paralyzed by what-ifs, may soon open for someone else who dared to knock, even with trembling hands.

Life rarely waits for you to be ready. It offers you windows, moments, tiny cracks in the wall where courage can squeeze through. If you don't move, those windows close. And while the world continues spinning, you're left wondering what might have happened if you had simply tried.

And so I ask you gently, but firmly, what are you waiting for? A sign? A guarantee? A version of yourself that feels less flawed, less human?

There is no perfect version. There is only *this* version, this flawed, unsure, hopeful version of you who is more capable than you realize, and who only needs to begin.

There's something sacred about a beginning. It's not polished, and it's rarely graceful, but it's pure. It's where courage and vulnerability meet in a fragile, beautiful mess. Starting isn't a weakness. It's a declaration: *I believe there's something in me worth growing.*

Even if you fail, even if you falter, even if you fumble every step of the way, that beginning still matters. It still transforms you.

Because every time you choose to act instead of shrink, you reclaim a little more power. You edge a little closer to who you're meant to be. And eventually, you stop asking, *Am I ready?* and start asking, *What am I waiting for?*

So go ahead, write the first messy sentence. Speak before your voice feels steady. Sign up. Show up. Begin. Not because you're sure you'll succeed, but because you know you'll grow either way.

Let fear walk beside you if it must, but don't let it decide your direction. The first step doesn't need to be perfect. It just needs to happen.

And maybe that's what readiness is, not the absence of fear, but the refusal to let fear dictate the shape of your life.

XI

To each their own

*"Some flowers bloom in spring,
Others in the hush of late September"*

How many times have you stopped yourself from sharing something that mattered to you, simply because you didn't think the other person would do the same? How often have you tucked away a thought, a feeling, or a truth, believing it was too much, too intense, too awkward, too *you* to be understood or welcomed?

It's subtle at first. The little ways you edit yourself in conversations. The softening of your voice when you're too afraid of sounding emotional. The way you shrink your excitement is because it might not be met with equal enthusiasm. Or the silence you swallow when something hurts, but you fear speaking it aloud would somehow burden the room.

These aren't just passing moments. Over time, they accumulate. You begin to question whether your feelings are valid at all. Whether your experiences deserve to be shared. Whether your voice matters, especially if others wouldn't offer theirs in return.

But where in that equation do *you* exist?

Where is the space where your heart gets to speak without editing itself? Where is the freedom to express joy, pain, confusion, excitement, *without* measuring it against how someone else might respond?

It took me a long time to realize that denying my voice didn't make me easier to love, it just made me disappear in my own story. And that's the quiet tragedy of self-abandonment. You begin by withholding a small part of yourself, but before you know it, you've contorted into someone unrecognizable. Someone palatable. Someone less "complicated."

But here's what I've learned, being too much, too deep, too honest, or too open is never the real problem. The problem is living in a world where we've been taught to believe that expressing who we are should come second to being accepted.

There is no honor in making yourself smaller so someone else can feel more comfortable. There is no reward for betraying your truth in exchange for someone's approval. You don't owe the world a quieter version of yourself just because others aren't willing to offer the same kind of vulnerability.

I've been there, sitting in silence, feeling like my thoughts were inconvenient. Holding back tears that wanted to be seen. Smiling when I felt like crumbling. And every time, I asked myself: *Would they do the same for me?*

And that question, though important, misses the point.

Because whether or not someone else shows up doesn't change the fact that *you* deserve to.

Your emotions aren't embarrassing. Your need to be heard isn't excessive. Your story isn't irrelevant just because someone else wouldn't have told it the same way. You are not here to be half of who you are so others don't feel overwhelmed by your fullness.

The truth is, people will come and go. They'll love you or they won't. They'll meet you halfway or leave you waiting. But at the end of every day, when the noise settles and the lights dim, the one person you'll always be with is *you*. And you owe that person everything.

So don't dim your light to blend in. Don't mute your truth to be digestible. And don't wait for others to validate what you know to be real. Speak, share, express, feel, *even if you're the only one in the room who understands it.* Because showing up as your full self is not a risk, it's a reclamation.

And you, just as you are, are worthy of that space.

Be unapologetically, wholeheartedly, unmistakably yourself. Not the watered-down version, not the version that fits in quietly at the table, not the one that's easier for others to digest. The real you, the one who feels things deeply, who carries beliefs close to their heart, who needs quiet days to breathe or loud ones to feel alive. That version deserves space.

If you believe in something, no matter how unconventional or misunderstood, stand by it. Let your values be your compass, even if the world around you doesn't always point in the same direction. If you cry often, let the tears fall without shame—they are not signs of weakness but proof that you care. And if you don't cry easily, that's not a flaw either. Feelings don't always look the same on everyone.

If you find joy in solitude, stay in. Light your candles, wear your comfiest clothes, and let the stillness be enough. If your peace is in your own space, protect it fiercely, no explanation required. You don't need to be the loudest in the room, the most adventurous, or the most outgoing to be complete. Who you are in your quietest, most unfiltered moments is already whole.

There is no prize for being more palatable. There is no gold star for molding yourself into someone else's comfort zone. The world doesn't need more copies, it needs more people willing to be themselves in a world that often tells them not to be. So, whatever makes you feel like you, your quirks, your silence, your storms, your softness, don't let go of it. That's your power. That's your truth. And that's more than enough.

XII

You're exactly where you're supposed to be

There's a strange kind of ache that comes with not knowing, with sitting in the in-between of who you were and who you're trying to become. It's the ache of walking forward without a map, of watching others seem so sure while you're still questioning if you even belong here. But maybe that ache isn't a sign that you're lost, maybe it's proof that you're paying attention. That you care. That you're awake enough to wonder if this life you're building is really yours.

I used to think certainty was the goal. That if I could just choose the "right" people, the "right" path, the "right" timing, everything would make sense. But what I've come to learn, slowly, painfully, beautifully, is that life doesn't hand us answers on a silver platter. It hands us moments. Fragments. Lessons wrapped in heartbreak. And it's our job to trust that even the hardest, quietest parts are preparing us for something we can't yet see.

Am I making the right choices?
Am I giving my time, my energy, my love to the right people?
Is this where I'm supposed to be? Do I even belong here at all?

These questions don't always shout. Most days, they echo softly, like background noise beneath the routine of it all, just loud enough to remind you they're still there. They creep in during the quiet moments, in the flicker of doubt before you fall asleep or the ache you feel when the day doesn't turn out the way you hoped. And no matter how much you grow, they return, because they're human questions. Soul-deep questions.

And we ask them not because we are broken, but because we care. Because we want to live with intention, to love with purpose, to walk paths that lead somewhere meaningful. We want to *get it right*. As if there's such a thing.

But the truth? Life rarely unfolds with clarity. It unfolds in layers. In false starts, detours, and unplanned reroutes. We want the blueprint, the confirmation that where we are is where we're meant to be, but sometimes, the map is still being drawn beneath our feet. And maybe that's not a flaw. Maybe that's the way it was always meant to be.

I think we forget that mystery is not the enemy of meaning. Some chapters are supposed to be messy, uncertain, and unfinished because if we had the full picture, we might never take that shaky first step. We'd cling to comfort, to certainty, and miss out on the messy, holy transformation that happens in the unknowing.

Maybe we're pulled away from what we thought was meant for us, not as punishment, but as preparation. Maybe the dream hasn't come true yet because we're still becoming the kind of person who can carry it with strength, with humility, with grace. Maybe the delay is divine, not because the vision was wrong, but because we're still growing into the hands that can hold it.

I'm 19. I'm not going to pretend I've cracked the code on any of this. In fact, this book is just me turning my questions into pages, hoping that in doing so, I'll stumble my way closer to clarity. But here's what I *do* know: you don't have to have it all figured out to belong. You just have to keep showing up, to your life, to your process, to yourself.

Life doesn't reward perfection, it rewards presence. It asks you to be your own anchor when the tides change, to be your own lighthouse when things go dark. And most of all, to be your own companion when the road feels lonely.

Letting go is one of the hardest things we ever do, especially when it involves people who once felt like home. But some loves are seasons, not lifetimes. And their ending doesn't make them less real. It just means their chapter in your story has closed, so a new one can begin.

There's a unique kind of grief that comes when you realize someone won't walk with you forever. Not because of betrayal or disaster, but because your paths no longer align. That quiet ache, the kind you carry without words, is real. And it deserves your tenderness.

So if you feel uncertain right now, if your heart feels unsteady or your direction unclear, please don't mistake it for failure. You're not unraveling. You're *unfolding*.

The most powerful lesson I've learned so far is this: trust doesn't mean knowing the outcome. It means believing there's meaning even in the confusion. Whether you call it God, the universe, fate, or simply the rhythm of time, trust that your life is not random. That even in the heartbreak, even in the silence, something sacred is being written.

Sometimes that belief will feel paper-thin. Sometimes you'll question it a hundred times in a single day. But hold onto it anyway. Let it be the fragile thread that pulls you through. Let it be the whisper that says, Keep going, even when everything inside you wants to stop.

Because even if you're standing in the middle of the storm right now, even if it feels like everything is falling apart, this isn't the end. It's the middle. It's the becoming.

And strangely, that's where the beauty is. I've found more peace in the chaos than I ever did in certainty. More meaning in the detours than in the plans that went "right." The bad days have taught me gratitude. The heartbreaks have softened me. And the uncertainty? It's taught me how to listen to my gut, to my heart, to the quiet knowing beneath it all.

So if today feels heavy, let it. If you're questioning everything, let yourself ask the questions. They won't break you. They'll build you.

And one day, maybe not soon but eventually, you'll look back and realize: the waiting, the wandering, the wondering, it was never wasted. You weren't just moving through time. You were becoming someone brave enough to live it.

You don't have to have it all figured out to be on the right path. You don't need every answer to be making progress. The truth is, the becoming never really ends. We're always shifting, growing, shedding, and learning to trust our feet even when the ground feels unfamiliar. So let this chapter be a reminder: your uncertainty is not a weakness, it's a whisper from the future, calling you forward. And you, even in your questions, even in your doubt, are already enough. You are not behind. You are not lost. You are simply becoming.

XIII

Love is never less

**"*Love is not louder when shouted.
It's just as real in the quiet ways we show up.*"**

We often talk about strength as if it only lives in loud places, in ambition, in hustle, in wins that can be posted or applauded. But there's a softer kind of strength that rarely makes headlines. It doesn't come with trophies or grand declarations. It doesn't seek the spotlight. But it carries us, shapes us, and moves us through the messiness of life.

That strength is love.

Not the kind we see in movies. Not the love wrapped in flowers and romantic tension. I'm talking about the quieter kind, the love between friends who stay, even when you're not at your best. The love of a parent who shows up, day after day, with no audience and no applause. The love you feel when a stranger smiles at you on a heavy day, or when someone you barely know sends a message that says, *"Just checking in."*

This kind of love doesn't make a lot of noise. But it builds empires within us.

It's the friend who listens to your silences without needing to fill them. The sibling who gets you in a way no one else can. The teacher who saw something in you before you could see it yourself. The mentor who told you that you mattered long before you believed it. These are the kinds of love that don't always get credited in your "success story", but they're the reason you made it through.

Love, in its purest form, is what steadies us when everything else feels unsteady. It reminds us we don't have to carry everything alone.

And this love, it doesn't always need words. Sometimes it shows up in the way someone saves you a seat. In the way your mom always asks if you've eaten. In the way, your friend knows exactly when you need a distraction and when you need space. It's in the consistent presence, the small gestures, the unspoken understanding.

I used to think love had to be grand to be real. That it had to be shouted from rooftops or written into song lyrics. But life has humbled me into seeing the opposite. Some of the most powerful kinds of love are the ones you almost overlook. They don't demand to be seen. They simply *are.*

And the more I've leaned into these kinds of love, the more I've realized, they're what keep us going. When the work gets hard. When the grind feels endless. When life asks you to stretch beyond what you think you're capable of. It's love that gets you through. Not motivation. Not pressure. Love.

Love for your family, who believe in you more than you believe in yourself. Love for your friends, who make life's weight feel lighter. Love for the version of you that you're trying to become. Love for your people, for your community, for something bigger than yourself.

Because love, in all its forms, fuels purpose.

When you're exhausted but still choose to show up, that's love. When you forgive, even when you could stay angry, that's love. When you make space for someone else's joy, even when yours feels far away, that's love. When you sit quietly with someone in their pain and don't try to fix it, that's love too.

And love like that? It's transformative. It ripples. It changes people in ways they might never be able to explain, but always remember.

We don't talk about this kind of love enough. But it's the love that teaches us patience, resilience, gentleness, and grit. It teaches us how to be better people. It's not perfect. It doesn't always show up the way we expect. But it's the foundation of the most beautiful parts of our lives.

So if you've ever wondered what's really holding you together when things fall apart, look closer. It might not be discipline. It might not be some five-year plan. It might just be love, in its quietest, truest form.

And maybe, just maybe, that's enough.

We don't always recognize it while we're in it, but love is often the quiet reason we keep going.

Not the fireworks kind. Not the kind that gets wrapped in neat labels. But the kind that looks like listening, like showing up, like holding space. The kind that's easy to miss until you need it most.

And maybe that's the whole point.

You don't need to have it all figured out. You don't need to run at full speed every day. Sometimes, the most honest work you'll ever do is learning how to receive love. How to give it freely. How to let it shape you, not into someone *perfect*, but into someone *present*.

So ask yourself gently:

- Who are the people in my life who love me quietly, without needing to be noticed?
- What kind of love have I been carrying that I haven't yet honored?
- Where does love show up in my daily life in ways I've overlooked?
- And how can I become someone who loves more intentionally, not just loudly, but deeply?

Let those questions sit with you. Write about them. Talk about them. Or just carry them with you into tomorrow.

Because no matter what life throws your way, you deserve to know this:

You are held.

You are carried.

You are loved.

And that love, unspoken, soft, unwavering, might just be the strongest thing in the world.

XIV
Even If No One Claps

*"Some of the most beautiful things bloom in silence.
And still, they bloom"*

There comes a point in every person's life, quiet and unannounced, where they are forced to look at themselves not through the polished lens of performance, but through the raw, unforgiving clarity of comparison. That aching moment when someone walks into a room and seems to carry something you don't. They speak effortlessly, move like light, and capture attention without asking for it. And you, standing beside them, begin to shrink without anyone asking you to.

It's a familiar ache, isn't it? The ache of *not enough*. Of watching someone else's highlights while replaying your behind-the-scenes. You might not even realize it's happening. It starts with the smallest thought: *Maybe if I were more like them...* And suddenly, you're no longer living from the inside out, you're performing from the outside in. You begin to trade in your softness for sleekness, your quiet for volume, your uncertainty for false confidence. You tell yourself you're evolving when in truth, you're erasing.

But here's what I've come to learn, through years of trying to become someone I thought would be more *palatable*: no one, not a single soul on this earth, can outdo you at being *you*. That isn't a consolation prize. That is a truth powerful enough to rebuild a life.

There is only one version of you in this sprawling, beautiful, imperfect universe. Just one. Your thoughts, your fears, your quirks, the songs you love, the way your voice rises when you're passionate, all of it, singular. All of it, sacred.

And yet, being yourself is one of the most radical and difficult things you'll ever do.

It means facing the parts of yourself you've been taught to hide, the awkwardness, the uncertainty, the dreamer who still believes in magic even when life tries to harden you. It means peeling away layers you've built just to survive, layers of sarcasm, perfectionism, self-deprecation, and daring to stand bare in your truth. It means saying: *I may not be the loudest in the room, but my presence still matters. I may not have it all figured out, but I still belong.*

For years, I thought strength looked like perfection. Like walking into a room and being undeniably magnetic, all sharp edges and confidence. But real strength, I've found, is far quieter. It's the courage to stay soft in a world that demands your armor. It's the decision to show up exactly as you are, without the mask. To hold your ground when you're tempted to morph into someone else. To say, *This is me. And that's enough.*

Comparison is a thief not only of joy, but of identity. It doesn't just rob you of happiness, it robs you of your*self.* And the danger of it is that it's often so quiet, so internal, you don't even notice it happening until one day, you realize you no longer recognize the person in the mirror. Not because you've grown, but because you've slowly, silently, disappeared.

It takes fierce intention to come back to yourself.

To unlearn the belief that your worth is tied to applause or aesthetics. To stop measuring your success by someone else's timeline. To reclaim your right to move at your own pace, speak in your own voice, and shape your life in your own rhythm.

This kind of self-return begins with awareness. With catching yourself mid-thought when you begin to doubt your value. By noticing how you shrink or shift when you're around certain people. And then, gently, without judgment, choosing a different response. Choosing to stay instead of run. Choosing to rest instead of hustle. Choosing to trust that even in your quietest moments, you are becoming.

Because the most painful kind of loneliness isn't being misunderstood by others, it's abandoning yourself in pursuit of being understood.

You fight battles every day that no one claps for. The small, internal victories, getting out of bed when everything inside you wants to stay under the covers, choosing grace over self-criticism, showing up to your life even when you feel invisible. That kind of quiet, persistent resilience is a strength the world doesn't always recognize, but it is powerful nonetheless.

We are taught to clap for others. To cheer for the milestones, the awards, the highlight reels. But we must learn to clap for ourselves too. For the quiet strength. For the days we choose to keep going. For the choice to be kind to ourselves when it would be easier to be cruel.

Loving yourself isn't some fluffy affirmation or hashtag, it is a radical act of resistance in a world that profits off your insecurity. It is choosing to see your flaws as facets. Your softness a power. Your contradictions as a human.

You don't owe the world a polished version of yourself. You owe yourself the freedom to be real.

So take the time to come home to yourself. Invest deeply. Not just in goals or aesthetics, but in rituals that feel like truth. Make your coffee the way you love it. Write late into the night if that's when your heart opens. Walk under trees that make you feel small in the best way. Sit in stillness without guilt. These things are not extras, they are anchors.

And when doubt visits you, as it always will, remember this: even the ones who seem the most certain still wonder if they're enough. What makes them different isn't that they're without fear. It's that they continue, anyway.

So continue. Choose you, again and again, even when it feels hard. Especially when it feels hard. Because the most powerful thing you will ever do in this life is become fully yourself.

You are not here to be like anyone else. You are here to be wholly, fiercely, unapologetically *you*.

And that—that is your superpower.

XV

Softness as Strength

In a world that spins fast and speaks loud, where applause often goes to the boldest, the fastest, the most visible, there is a kind of power that rarely makes headlines. It doesn't flash across screens or flood your feed. It doesn't demand attention or compete for the spotlight. It doesn't win races or break records. But it changes everything.

Kindness.

Not the curated kind. Not the kind wrapped in hashtags or captured for applause. I'm talking about the kind that's unspoken, almost invisible, the kind that lives in the smallest, most tender corners of everyday life. The kind that no one may notice, except the person who receives it... and the soul that gave it.

We talk so much about strength, about ambition, about chasing dreams with grit and fire. But rarely do we speak about kindness as a form of courage. About the strength it takes to stay soft in a world that keeps trying to harden you. About the bravery required to respond to cruelty with compassion, to meet rejection with understanding, to choose gentleness over retaliation.

Kindness is often underestimated, perhaps because it doesn't always come with a payoff. It doesn't offer guarantees. You can pour your heart into being good to people, and still be misunderstood. You can choose softness, and still be hurt. And yet, the quiet beauty of kindness lies in its resilience, it gives anyway. It chooses grace, even when grace isn't returned. It keeps going, not because it expects something back, but because it knows the value of giving.

Think of all the small, almost forgettable moments that stayed with you: the teacher who noticed when you were having a bad day. The friend who texted you at midnight just to say they believed in you. The stranger who held the door when your hands were full. The sibling who sat with you in silence when words felt too heavy.

We carry those moments, don't we?

Even when we forget the details, the feeling lingers. Kindness leaves fingerprints on our hearts.

And yet, somehow, we still treat kindness as an afterthought, a luxury to offer when everything else is done. But what if it were the foundation? What if, instead of treating it as a bonus, we treated it as the baseline?

The truth is, we don't know the battles others are fighting. Most people are walking through invisible wars, carrying griefs we'll never see. And sometimes, the simplest act of consideration, a kind word, a moment of patience, a genuine smile, can be the thing that pulls someone back from the edge. It costs nothing. But its value is immeasurable.

But here's where it gets harder, and where I want to linger a little longer.

We're taught, from a young age, to be kind to others. To share our toys. To say "please" and "thank you." To forgive, to include, to show empathy. But how many of us were taught to direct that same tenderness inward?

When was the last time you gave yourself the grace you offer so freely to others?

We speak so harshly to ourselves, far more harshly than we ever would to a friend. We pick ourselves apart for the slightest misstep. We replay our mistakes like broken records, whispering to ourselves that we should have done better, should have known better, should have been more.

But you are not a machine. You are not a project to be fixed. You are a living, breathing human being, flawed and miraculous and learning as you go. And you deserve your own compassion.

Self-kindness is not indulgence. It is not laziness or weakness. It is necessary. Vital. Foundational. Because the way you speak to yourself becomes the filter through which you experience the world. If you walk through life believing you are not enough, everything you encounter will confirm it. But if you practice grace, real, messy, imperfect grace, then even in your darkest moments, you'll have a light.

I write this not from a place of mastery, but of deep knowing. I've stood in front of mirrors and winced. I've compared my behind-the-scenes to someone else's highlight reel. I've let my inner critic become a dictator, convincing me I was falling behind, that I wasn't lovable, that I hadn't done enough.

But I've also had moments—quiet, precious moments, where I chose differently. I spoke to myself gently. I let the tears come without judgment. I sat with my mess and said, "You're still worthy. Even here."

That is the beginning of something sacred.

When we practice kindness toward ourselves, something inside us shifts. We become less reactive, more open. We begin to hold space for others without losing ourselves in the process. We give not from emptiness, but from overflow. And that kind of giving, the kind that doesn't deplete you, is the most sustainable, soul-deep love there is.

So let kindness be your rebellion. Let it be your quiet revolution in a world that glorifies competition and critique. Let it be the language you speak to your younger self, your future self, your hurting self. Let it guide the way you speak to others, yes, but more importantly, let it transform the way you speak to yourself.

Not every moment will be perfect. Not every day will feel gentle. But each time you choose kindness toward the world, toward others, toward yourself, you are rewriting what it means to be strong.

And maybe that's the legacy worth leaving. Not a resume of achievements or a list of milestones, but a trail of softness in hard places. A record of warmth in cold spaces. A history of choosing love when it wasn't easy.

Because in the end, it's not the noise we made that will be remembered. It's the comfort we offered. The space we created. The grace we embodied.

It's the kindness we gave when no one was looking.

And that, I believe, is what holds the world together.

XVI
LONG LIVE FAITH

**_"Faith is the whisper that remains
even after the world has gone quiet"_**

Ever since I was little, my mother would say with unwavering conviction, "Hold your faith strong, through anything and everything." She spoke those words like they were a shield, an invisible armor meant to protect me through every stage of life. I'd nod, half-understanding, brushing it off like the way children do with most things they don't fully grasp. Back then, faith felt simple, almost tangible. It wasn't something abstract or spiritual, it was my mother's embrace after a hard day, my father's presence in the room when I was scared of the dark. As children, our faith is personified in the people who love us. We believe in their ability to fix things, to make the world feel right again.

But life, as it does, changes shape. And with it, so did my understanding of what faith really means. Somewhere between growing up and growing through, I realized that faith isn't always about knowing. It's not about having the answers or even being sure of the outcome. It's about trusting, trusting in God, in the universe, in timing, and in the unseen currents that carry us forward when our own strength isn't enough. We're taught to believe in effort, in plans, in control, but control is, more often than not, an illusion dressed as security. And in the absence of control, belief becomes our anchor.

When believing in yourself feels like too tall an order, when your reflection seems unfamiliar and your voice echoes with doubt, sometimes, all you can do is believe in something greater than yourself. Believe in divine timing. Believe in a purpose not yet visible. Believe that the chaos is making room for clarity.

If I'm honest, my relationship with faith hasn't been graceful. It's been messy, flawed, and a little bit comical, like trying to steady a kite in a hurricane. For a long time, I pretended I didn't expect much from life. It was easier to convince myself that disappointment didn't sting if you never hoped to begin with. I called it realism, but in truth, it was a carefully constructed defense mechanism. I buried my desires under a pile of cynicism, believing that if I never admitted what I truly wanted, it wouldn't hurt so badly when it didn't come to pass. But somewhere beneath all of that was still a very human longing, to win, to be chosen, to succeed. And when things didn't work out, I'd blame fate, like it was some unfair dealer in a rigged game.

That worked for a while. Until it didn't.

Because eventually, life cornered me. Everything I thought I had figured out began unraveling at once, and I was left staring at the pieces, completely unsure of how to put them back together. I couldn't control the damage. I couldn't will things into place. And in that quiet, terrifying moment of surrender, when I had no option but to let life unfold however it chose, I finally began to understand faith. Not as a certainty. But as a choice.

Letting go sounds poetic when written on a page, but in practice, it can be one of the most excruciating things we're called to do. It requires patience, vulnerability, and the ability to sit in the discomfort of not knowing. There's a strange kind of strength, though, in choosing to wait. In resisting the urge to control. In believing that if we've done the work, if we've poured our hearts into the process, then maybe the rest isn't up to us. Maybe the magic isn't in making things happen, but in allowing them to.

To me, faith isn't about idly waiting for miracles to drop from the sky. It's about whispering to yourself, even on your worst days, "I've done what I can, and now I release the rest." It's the quiet courage to trust that the path you're walking, though foggy and winding, is still leading somewhere meaningful.

And if what you're hoping for doesn't arrive? If things fall apart despite your best efforts? Then maybe, just maybe, it's because you were meant for something even greater than what you were asking for. Something your heart hasn't even imagined yet.

I'm not here to tell you what to believe in. Faith isn't something you can force, and it certainly isn't something that blooms on command. It finds you.

Sometimes in the aftermath of loss. Sometimes in a moment of stillness. Sometimes when life has brought you to your knees and you have nowhere left to turn. And it teaches you, often through pain, that your job is not to control the outcome, but to stay open, to keep showing up, to keep believing that your effort is never in vain.

We carry so much. So much pressure to perform, to succeed, to hold it all together. But the truth is, not everything was meant to be held. Some things are meant to be released. Some burdens are not yours to carry. And it's only when you learn to distinguish between the two that you begin to reclaim your peace.

Faith is not an escape from reality. It's a decision to move through life with open eyes and a willing heart. It's the steady whisper beneath the noise, reminding you that even if nothing makes sense right now, it doesn't mean it never will. You are not failing just because things are unclear. You're becoming. And becoming takes time.

So loosen your grip. Soften your heart. Let go of what you thought it had to look like. Life will rarely match your timelines, but it will always teach you something valuable along the way. The truth is, the most beautiful things are often born in the waiting, in that strange, in-between place where you're no longer who you were, but not yet who you're becoming.

Trust that what's meant for you will find its way, in its own time, in its own form. And what isn't meant for you? No amount of pleading or pushing will make it stay. There's a quiet power in knowing that. In choosing to focus on what's within your control, your effort, your integrity, your growth, and leaving the rest to something greater.

Let that be enough. Let that be faith.

XVII
Live a little

"Somewhere between striving and stillness,
You get to decide what living means."

Everywhere we look, the world chants a relentless anthem: go harder. Wake earlier. Work later. Fill the silence. Monetize your hobbies. Document your milestones. Don't stop until you've earned rest, and even then, ask yourself if you've earned it enough.

This is the culture we've inherited, one that glorifies the hustle and vilifies the pause. One that tells us we must always be doing, achieving, performing. Rest becomes something we feel guilty about. Stillness becomes synonymous with stagnation. We are constantly told to be "more": more productive, more ambitious, more seen. But I've come to believe that there's another way. A quieter, slower, and perhaps more sacred one.

At 19, I am not wise in the conventional sense. I don't have all the answers, and I don't pretend to. But I do know this much: we were not made to burn at both ends. We were not created to be machines of output, chasing an ever-moving finish line. We are not just what we accomplish, we are who we are when the noise fades. When we're alone with ourselves, with nothing to prove and no one to impress.

There's a quote I once clung to: *"Do it even when you have no reason to, that's reason enough."* And for a long time, I let that quote carry me through the fog. I wore it like armor on the days when motivation was nowhere to be found, when my dreams felt distant and my energy ran thin. But if I'm being honest, I also wrestled with it. Because some days, I didn't want to "do it."

Some days, I didn't want to push through or show up or strive. I didn't want to keep proving that I was strong.

Some days, I just wanted permission to be.

And maybe that's what this final chapter is: permission. To soften. To stop. To exhale. To reclaim the parts of yourself that the world keeps asking you to trade in for productivity.

We live in a world that tells us we're wasting time if we aren't constantly optimizing it. But there is no such thing as wasted time when you are learning how to love being in your own company. There is no wasted time when you're resting, healing, growing, especially if the world has convinced you that rest is laziness, that healing is indulgent, that growth only counts if it's visible.

The truth is, we all crave a sense of enough-ness. We want to know that our lives are meaningful, that our days matter, that we're not falling behind. But balance isn't a finish line you cross once and for all. It's not a perfectly measured equation. It's a relationship you build with yourself, a daily negotiation between effort and ease, between ambition and gentleness.

Some seasons will be chaotic. They'll demand more of you. They'll stretch you thin. But others? Others will be quieter. Slower. Sacred in their softness. These are the seasons that ask you not to chase, but to listen. Not to build, but to rebuild. And those seasons matter just as much.

It took me a long time to realize that I don't need to earn rest. That joy, too, is a valid goal. That fun is not frivolous, and that presence is a kind of productivity no one talks about enough. These days, I try not to measure the quality of my life by how much I've done, but by how much of myself I've reclaimed in the process.

If your joy looks different than someone else's, that's okay. If your ambition whispers instead of shouts, honor it. If the way you choose to live your life doesn't fit the mold, good. You weren't made to fit in; you were made to come home to yourself.

Fun is a chapter. Joy is a spark. But depth, that's the foundation. And the most fulfilling life is one built on both: the glitter and the grounding, the noise and the quiet, the laughter in a crowded room and the peace in your own presence.

So let this final chapter be your gentle reminder: You are allowed to slow down. You are allowed to be still. You are allowed to take up space without proving your worth through exhaustion. You are allowed to be a work in progress and still be whole.

You don't need to chase the world. It will be there. But you? You only get this one heart, this one life, this one chance to write your story on your own terms.

Let it be soft in the places that need softening. Let it be bold where it wants to be bold. Let it rest when it's tired. Let it rise again when it's ready.

And most of all, let it be yours.

"WHERE THE WORDS BEGIN AGAIN"

So here we are, at the end, and also, the beginning.

There's something sacred about endings, not because they're final, but because they ask us to reflect. To look back at where we started, to notice the miles we've quietly walked, the pieces we've picked up, the versions of ourselves we've outgrown along the way. This book began in uncertainty, in questions, in the ache of becoming, and maybe it ends there too. But this time, the uncertainty doesn't feel so heavy. This time, it feels like freedom.

If you're still trying to figure out who you are, what you want, where you're going—good. That means you're still alive, still growing, still listening to the parts of yourself that whisper instead of shout. That means you haven't settled for noise in place of meaning. That means you're human.

If there's one truth I hope you carry from these pages, it's this: your life does not need to look like anyone else's to be meaningful. You are allowed to walk slowly. To change your mind. To pause. To begin again. You are allowed to grow in the quiet, away from the spotlight, and still be proud of what you're becoming.

You don't need to chase the version of yourself the world expects. You only need to return, again and again, to the version that feels most like home.

And maybe, just maybe, that's what this life is really about. Not perfecting every chapter, but writing them with honesty. Not racing to the end, but learning to live inside each sentence. Fully. Deeply. Unapologetically.

Let this be your reminder: you are not behind. You are not broken. You are not too much or not enough. You are becoming, beautifully, slowly, precisely as you're meant to.

So go gently. Go bravely. Go as you are.

"Maybe you won't have all the answers.
Maybe you won't always feel ready.
But you'll always have a page to return to,
and a self-worth writing about."
  -*Where the words begin, may they always bring you back to yourself.*